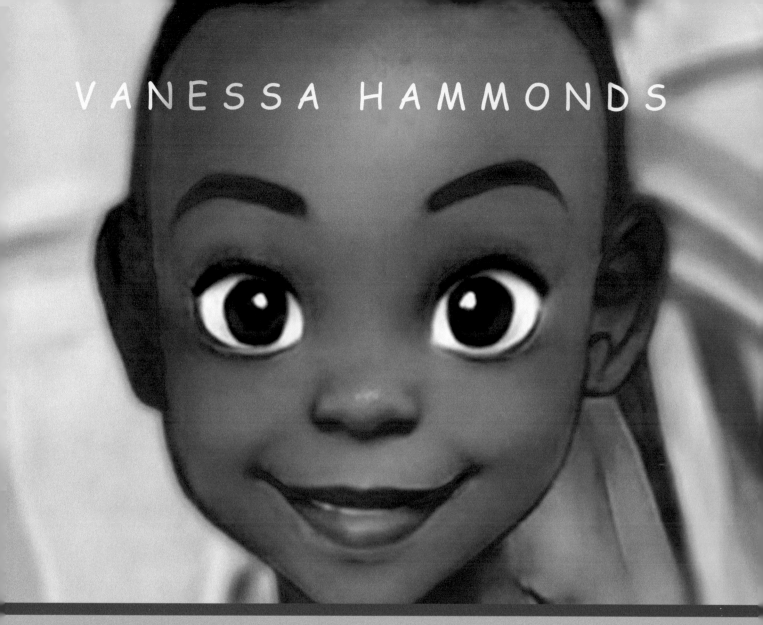

VANESSA HAMMONDS

BROWN
PAPER BAG

~A story about culture, exploration, and imagination~

To order additional copies of this book, contact:
Xlibris
844-714-8691
www.Xlibris.com
Orders@Xlibris.com

ISBN: 978-1-6641-8903-4 (sc)
ISBN: 978-1-6641-8903-4 (e)

Print information available on the last page

Rev. date: 08/27/2021

"BROWN PAPER BAG"

~A story about culture, exploration, and imagination~

Written by Vanessa "Nes" Hammonds

Illustrated by Zhiyana Hammonds

Africa, Aruba, China, Australia, France! I want to go to every Country; I must get the chance.

I am Brielle, an explorer to be, I sit in my room and play make believe, my brown paper bag is magical you see, Whenever I look inside, I am in a different Country!

Up first, a beautiful beach and a Divi-Divi tree! I don't know where I could be, the water behind me makes me want to swim and scuba but where am I... I know! I'm in Aruba!!

That was a great swim, but it feels good to be on land.

Where's my brown paper bag. Oh wait! There it is! Buried in the sand.

I dig and dig finally, I look inside, I'm so excited to go on another ride! I'm flying and swinging and suddenly I stop!

Everything looks so different.; the language, the food, the way we are dressed.

I must say, I am quite impressed! Where am I? I haven't a clue, what I see are pangolin and bamboo.

I keep exploring as I
take a leisure walk, I
see tons a building oh
so tall.

Ahh I am in China! I
see its Great wall!

My brown paper bag is in my hand, let's look in to travel to another land

I am here, but where? Let's find out!
There are Kangaroos and Koalas are
moving about. The sun is beaming, the
weather is hot and dry, rainbow lorikeets,
echidnas, and dingoes are wondering by.

The staple food here is the meat pie, I am going to try it if I can. Did you guess where I am?

If you guessed Australia, you're right! I am!

The sandstorm took my brown paper bag and I to a different country, one where the food smells so good, it is making me hungry!

Macarons, Tarte Tatin, Crepes, and Baguettes, what country am I in? I haven't figured it out yet.

All the sights are oh so pretty, there is a ton of monumental buildings and towers and the weather is windy. The natives greet you by saying "Bonjour"

am I in Africa? No, I am in France and that's for sure!

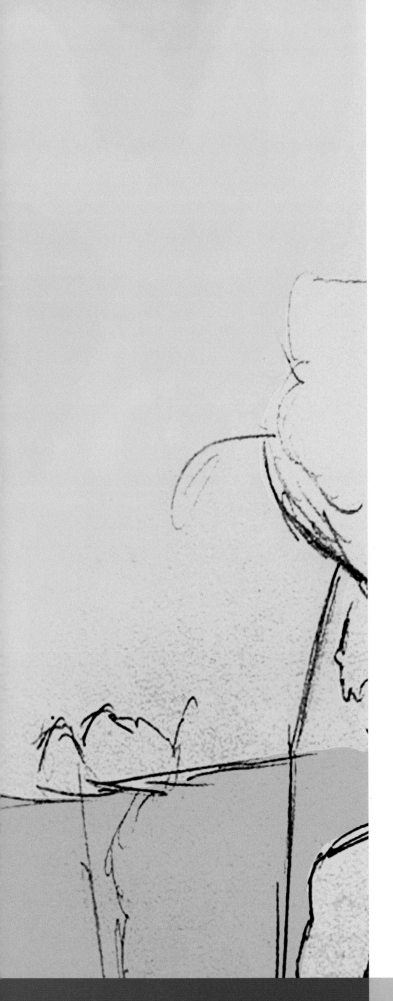

Landing on different ground, such a beautiful sight all around. I see a bunch of wildlife and hear all sorts of bird calls.

I'm standing beside Victoria Falls, the natives call it "mosi-oa-tunya", one of the most beautiful sights in Africa!

- My brown paper bag takes me everywhere that I can imagine. Different ways to learn are closer than it seems just read, explore and play make believe.

- Wherever you want to go and whatever you want to do, believe in yourself. It's all up to you!

ABOUT THE BOOK

"Brown paper bag" is a story about adventure, imagination, and culture. Brielle is a seven year old girl that loves to travel, read and explore. Every time she looks into her brown paper bag, she is whisked away to another country. Take a journey with Brielle and learn about different, animals, foods, dressing styles, and monuments of different countries!

Printed in the United States
by Baker & Taylor Publisher Services